The One and Only Bunbun

by SUSAN CLYMER

illustrated by ATI FORBERG

SCHOLASTIC INC.
New York Toronto London Auckland Sydney

With love
to Trudie Heming . . .
who lived many of these adventures

ISBN 0-590-32463-2

Copyright © 1983 by Susan Clymer. Illustrations © 1983 by Scholastic Inc. All rights reserved. Published by Scholastic Inc.

12 11 10 9 8 7 6 5   2 3/9
                                                              28
Printed in the U.S.A.

Bunbun Arrives

Terri stuffed the half-peeled Easter egg into her basket and raced down the stairs after Jason. Her older brother flung open the door. "There's no one here," he said.

A small, white, fluffy rabbit hopped across the mat. Terri ducked under Jason's arm and knelt in front of it.

"A rabbit rang the doorbell?" Jason asked.

The rabbit had pink eyes and a pink nose that twitched. Terri held out her hands, and the little rabbit hopped to her. "It likes me," she said. Gently, she picked it up and held it in the crook of her right elbow. For as long as she could remember, Terri had wanted a pet. Maybe she could have a rabbit.

"But where did it come from? Someone must have brought it." Jason searched behind the bushes along the house.

Terri brushed her fingers along the rabbit's shoulders. Its fur felt softer than cotton balls. "Bunbun," she said softly. "If you were mine, I would name you Bunbun."

"Ruth!" Jason pulled their baby-sitter out from behind the hedge. "*You* left the rabbit on our doorstep!"

"Is Bunbun — I mean the rabbit — a present?" Terri asked Ruth.

Ruth nodded. "He's for you and Jason."

"For me?" Terri's cry made the rabbit's ears shoot up in alarm. His eyes stretched wide.

"Bunbun is a baby name," Jason said.

Terri ignored him. She clutched the little rabbit against her chest and ran up the stairs to her parents' bedroom. "Mom! Dad!" She rushed into the room, forgetting to knock. "Ruth brought an Easter present. A rabbit for me." Then she added, "And Jason."

Her parents sat up in bed.

Terri held the rabbit out in front of her. "Look, he's beautiful." Bunbun quivered. Two small droppings fell and landed on the floor.

"We'll come down in a few minutes and discuss it," her mother said. She sounded upset.

Terri knew that "discussing it" always meant no. Every time she wanted a pet, her mother said no. "Can't I keep him?" Terri wailed.

"Go on. Out." Her father gently shooed her from the room.

"And keep that creature outside," her mother called.

Terri stomped down the steps and grabbed her coat. It was cold in

Maine, even in April. She could hear her brother and Ruth playing catch, but she wanted to be alone. She sat down under the kitchen window and put the rabbit on the ground.

Bunbun twitched his nose and hopped. Terri reached for him, but he changed direction almost in midair. The white rabbit zigzagged halfway across the lawn until Terri ran in front of him, and he froze.

Terri picked up the rabbit and held him firmly. She sat back down against the kitchen wall and formed a circle with her legs in front of her. Then she stuffed the empty places under her knees with the bottom of her coat. She put Bunbun down in the middle of the circle. He was so small he couldn't hop out.

The kitchen window squeaked open above Terri's head. "I don't want to keep that rabbit," her mother's voice insisted. "We both know who would end up taking care of it."

"I'm sure Terri could manage by herself." Her father's voice was calm.

Terri stood up. She wanted to hear every word. The window was open just a crack, and steam poured out. The teapot began to whistle. The whistle was so loud she couldn't hear her father talking. She counted all the way to five before someone took the pot off the stove. She heard her father's voice again. ". . . pretty harmless. Besides, the droppings will give me a good start on my compost heap."

"You sound as if you want to keep it," her mother said.

"Terri has always wanted a pet," her father answered. "It's better than a cat or a dog."

The rabbit squeaked, and Terri realized she was clutching him too tightly.

Her mother sighed. "Well, it will probably die in a couple of weeks anyway. Easter animals always do. We'll keep the rabbit."

"Hooray!" Terri cried. The window opened wide, and her father's head poked out.

"Were you eavesdropping?" he asked gruffly, but he didn't seem angry.

"No, sir, I was just listening," she said. Her father laughed. Terri felt her face grow red. Her father pulled his head in and closed the window.

"Daddy," she yelled, "Bunbun will live forever."

Smuggling the Rabbit

That night, the door to Terri's bedroom opened with a *click*. Terri pretended to be asleep. *Maybe I should snore*, she thought. The idea of snoring made her almost laugh out loud. She made a small hiccuping sound.

Through a tiny opening in her eyelids, she watched her mother take two steps toward her bed and peer at her. Terri forced herself to breathe evenly. *In—two—three—four. Out— two—three—four* she counted in her head over and over again. Each time she breathed, she took in more air than she could let out. Her lungs felt as if they were going to pop. Then her left big toe itched, and she wanted to scratch it.

Finally her mother left the room and closed the door behind her. Terri let her breath out with a *whoosh*.

A few minutes later, Terri put on her robe and slippers and looked out the keyhole. The hallway was dark. "I'm coming, Bunbun," she whispered and turned the knob. When she pulled, the door creaked. Terri waited, then gently pulled again. *Crreeeaaaakkkkk*. She slipped out. There was no light under her parents' door.

Terri tiptoed down the stairs. She stayed close to the banister. Just this morning Jason had shown her that the edge of the stairs didn't squeak as much as the middle.

Next she had to feel her way across the dining room. But that was easy. One of her favorite games was pretending she was blind and walking around with her eyes shut.

A ray of moonlight fell across the kitchen floor. Terri knelt by a wooden crate. That afternoon Terri had cut the end off a shoe box. Then she had put the box in one corner of Bunbun's crate. She expected him to be hiding there now. But the rabbit sat in the middle of the crate, staring at her.

"Poor lonely bunny," she said softly and tucked him into the crook of her arm. She started back to her bedroom. This time she could see where she was going. Maybe her eyes were getting used to the dark.

Terri crept up the stairs, almost to the top. She heard a door open. Her father walked across the landing to the bathroom. Terri held her breath and stood as still as she could. Her father stumbled sleepily past her. But he never turned his head.

Terri sneaked into her room and shut the door. "We made it, Bunbun." She put him down on the end of the bed.

Terri slipped off her robe and crawled in between the covers. Bunbun hopped up to her shoulders. "We'll do this every night," she said. "You'll never have to stay in that kitchen alone again. But I have to get you back before Mom wakes up." Terri draped her right arm around the little rabbit and fell asleep.

Terri opened her eyes slowly. She stared at a small white head with a twitching pink nose. Sunlight filled the room. "Bunbun!" Terri giggled and tickled his tail.

She heard the teapot whistling in the kitchen. "Mom is awake!" Terri sat straight up in bed. "How am I going to get you back now?"

There were little brown rabbit droppings all over her blue quilt. "Oh, no!" she groaned. Terri doubled over the hem of her nightgown to make a pocket. She picked up all the droppings and headed for the bathroom.

She closed her bedroom door and walked slowly, careful not to spill anything.

"Good morning, Terri." Her mother came up the stairs and gave her a hug. "What do you have in your nightgown?"

Terri stared at her. She couldn't say a word.

"And where did you get that hole in

your sleeve?" her mother demanded.

Terri looked at her arm and said, "Oh, no, the rabbit." Then she was so horrified that she dropped the hem of her nightgown. Pellets rolled across the floor.

"Terri, do you have that rabbit in your room?" Her mother started for the bedroom.

Terri ran ahead of her and opened the door. She was just in time to see Bunbun hop from the bed to the nightstand. He lost his balance and slid across the nightstand into the lamp. Terri heard her mother gasp. The lamp wobbled and crashed to the floor.

Bunbun's Snack

"Why don't you call him Peter?" Jason asked.

It was a warm spring day, almost a month later. Terri sat on the ground beside the rabbit cage. "His name is Bunbun," she answered.

Terri opened the little screen door in the cage just enough to poke a carrot through. Bunbun gnawed the carrot away. His lips felt fuzzy against her fingertips. Terri liked the wooden cage. Her father had built a slanted roof just like the roof on their house. Then he had put in a screen bottom to keep Bunbun off the ground.

"What about Jack for jackrabbit?" her father suggested. He was turning over the hard ground with a shovel to plant some pansies.

"Or Simon, or anything but Bunbun!" Jason exclaimed.

Terri grinned, but didn't answer. Sometimes she liked to upset her brother.

"That rabbit is almost cute as an outdoor pet." Her mother leaned out the kitchen window.

Terri still wished Bunbun could stay inside with her at night. But keeping him outdoors was better than giving him away.

A strange woman walked into the yard. "Hi, Gwin," she said to Terri and Jason's mother. She nodded to their father, and then, to Terri's surprise, knelt in front of the cage. "Nice rabbit you have.

"I'm Dr. Williams." The woman

shook hands with Terri and then Jason. "I'm a veterinarian, an animal doctor." She wore a brown blouse with a picture of an orange cat above the pocket. "Your mother asked me to come check the rabbit over. May I pick him up?"

Terri looked at the doctor's friendly face. Her mother hated animals, and her father laughed at them. But Dr. Williams seemed different. "Sure," Terri said.

Dr. Williams unhooked the latch and pulled the rabbit out of the cage. "Never pick him up by his ears," she told Terri. "Grab him by the back of the neck and put the other hand under his bottom." Bunbun kicked with his back feet, and the doctor laughed. "Feisty fellow. You may have this rabbit for years."

Jason groaned. "Bunbun. I'll have to listen to that name for years?"

Terri started to kick Jason, but her

father's hands came down on each of their shoulders.

"He's healthy?" Her mother sounded surprised. "But Easter pets are never healthy. There *must* be something wrong with him."

"Not this rabbit." Dr. Williams pulled a leash and a bright yellow collar out of her pocket. She hooked the collar around Bunbun's neck and handed him to Terri. "The rabbit needs exercise. But you had better keep him on a leash until he gets bigger."

"Why?" Terri asked.

"So a cat doesn't get him."

Jason giggled.

Terri put Bunbun on the ground. He hopped backward. He jerked his head and twirled in the air. Then he dashed in a straight line toward the bushes at the side of the house. Terri had to run to keep up with him.

"Thank you," she called over her shoulder, and Dr. Williams smiled.

Bunbun hopped behind the bushes, so Terri had to crawl. The rabbit zipped across the lawn to the hedge. A bicycle came along the road, and Bunbun froze. Then he nibbled on some grass, hopped a few steps, and nibbled some more. Terri followed him all the way around the house.

Her dad was still working with his shovel, but everyone else had left.

"I'm going inside for a while, Dad," she said. Her pants were muddy and damp from crawling behind the bushes. She took the collar off Bunbun and opened his cage.

"Leave him out," her father said. "I'll watch for any cats."

Terri opened the back door. She heard her mother working in the living room. Terri sneaked up the stairs. Her mother would yell at her if she saw her dirty clothes.

Terri changed into her favorite bright blue pants and looked out the window down into the backyard.

Her father was planting the pansies. He dug a hole, put a plant in, and patted the ground around it. Then he took a step, dug a hole, and planted another one.

By the time he put the third plant in the ground, Bunbun hopped over to sniff the pansies. The rabbit chomped the first plant all the way to the ground.

Terri watched Bunbun jump to the second plant and begin to nibble. Her father never once looked behind him.

Terri tried to open the window. It was stuck. She banged on the pane, but her father didn't even turn his head. He went right on planting pansies. The rabbit hopped along behind him, eating them all.

Terri ran down the stairs and out to the backyard. "Dad!" she yelled.

But her father had finished planting. He had just turned around to look at his row of pansies. Bunbun stared up at him with a golden flower sticking out of his mouth. That was the only plant in sight.

Her father yelled. He waved his trowel in the air and jumped up and down. Bunbun sat still. The rabbit slowly chewed until the last petal had disappeared.

Rabbit for Dinner

Bunbun was growing every day. He didn't fit into the crook of Terri's elbow anymore. She held him in both arms.

"Come on. It's time to go," her mother called. The whole family was going to Grandma's for a reunion.

Terri nuzzled her face down into Bunbun's warm fur. How could she leave him for two days? He would miss her. She spent part of every day with him. "I'll be back," she mumbled and put him in his cage.

The day after Bunbun had eaten the pansies, her father had brought home an old collie run so Bunbun could exercise himself. The run was a big pen made out of wire with a roof as tall as Terri. The rabbit's little wooden hutch sat in one corner. Bunbun pressed his nose up against the wire.

Terri ran to the car and scrambled into the back seat beside Jason. She watched silently as they drove through the city.

When they reached the country, Jason began to sing, "Oh, my darling, oh, my darling . . ."

Terri joined him. But she sang, "Oh, my doctor, Clementine," just as she had when she was four years old.

Her father grinned at her.

Hours later, her mother turned the car into the dirt road that led to Grandma's house. Terri rolled down the window and stuck her head out. The air smelled fresh and piney. A small brown animal hopped out from behind a bush and froze. "A rabbit!" Terri cried. "Grandma has rabbits, too."

Her mother stopped the car in front of Grandma's house. Uncle John sat on the porch with a gun across his lap. "Going hunting," he said as they got out of the car. "Anybody want to come?"

Jason went with him, but Terri followed her mother into the house. She couldn't bear being around when Uncle John brought the birds home to clean for dinner. He'd stand by that old pump and pull out the feathers. One time he had even brought home a deer. Terri had come across him by mistake while he was skinning it. Today she would just stay inside.

Grandma's house didn't have any electricity. The family thought she was crazy not to put electricity in when her neighbors did. Terri guessed Grandma just liked living this way. There wasn't even a toilet, just an outhouse with a shiny white toilet seat.

Most of Terri's uncles and aunts and a few cousins were in the living room already, but there was no one near her age.

Terri went into the kitchen for some water. She put a bucket under the tap and pumped up and down on the old wooden handle. Then she scooped the water out of the bucket with a cup and poured it into a glass. "Want some, Mom?" She poured out another glassful. The water tasted good here.

"When I was a little girl about your age, my chore used to be keeping the fire going in this old stove." Her mother opened a small door in the side of the stove. "See, you put wood in here and that heats the oven and the burners."

"Let's go up to your old bedroom,"

Terri said. She was surprised when her
mother agreed. They climbed the giant
stairs hand in hand. Terri had to
stretch to make each step. Two big

rooms opened off the top of the stairs. "One for the girls and one for the boys." Terri dragged her mother through a doorway. "And this was your bed." Terri grabbed a cornerpost and pulled herself onto the high bed. She held the soft pillow against her stomach.

"That pillow is made of goose down." Her mother sat beside her. "I collected the down for the pillow all by myself."

Terri leaned her head against her mother's shoulder. Usually all they did was argue. It was nice to just talk to her mom.

That evening, Terri helped set the table for dinner. She folded each cloth napkin differently. She made a triangle, a square, and even a letter M for her mother.

Finally the family sat down to eat. Terri was starving. She took some mashed potatoes and made a perfect well in the middle for gravy. Jason passed a platter of meat, and Terri speared a few hunks. It smelled different. "What kind of meat is this?" she asked.

No one heard her.

"Uncle John," she said, louder this time. "What is this meat?"

"Rabbit, child," he said proudly. "Fresh rabbit."

Terri looked at her plate, then at her uncle, and screamed, "Rabbit!"

The fifteen people around the table were instantly silent. Her mother glared at her. "Terri, eat your dinner."

"It's rabbit!" she cried. She hoped her mother would understand. "Mom, how could you eat rabbit?"

"Terri . . ." her father warned.

Terri shoved back her chair, stood up, and pointed her finger at Uncle John. "You killed a rabbit!"

"Terri, it's not Bunbun," Jason said, but he looked a little sick.

Terri glared at Uncle John. "But it might be Bunbun's cousin, or even his rotten *uncle*."

Her mother grabbed her arm and pushed her toward her seat. Terri jerked free. "No, Mother," she screamed, "I won't eat rabbit!" Her father stood up. Terri ran to the front door. "I won't even stay in the same house with people who eat rabbits!" She slammed the door behind her and burst into tears.

Terri climbed into the car behind the steering wheel. She spent a long time thinking about how much she hated everyone. Finally, Jason came out of the house with a peanut butter sandwich. "Here," he said.

"Thanks," Terri mumbled. But she knew even Jason had eaten rabbit.

Flying Rabbit

One September afternoon, Terri lay on her back in the cool grass. She looked up at the oak tree. Fall was her favorite season. The leaves were turning color. A few were still green, but most were different shades of red. A red leaf tinged with brown drifted off the tree and spun down onto her shoulder. Terri picked up the leaf and twirled the stem in her fingers.

"Jason, can you smell the storm?" she asked. "The air smells wet."

"It is, silly. Hurricane Hazel is coming."

Terri raised herself on her elbows. "The birds are quiet. Look at Bunbun!"

The rabbit sat completely still in the corner of his pen, his ears up, his eyes wide. A rising wind blew Terri's hair away from the sides of her face. Bun-bun bolted for his wooden house.

"He will be safe there," Jason said. "We'd better go inside, too."

A drop of rain landed on the back of Terri's neck. She took one last look at the rabbit cage and ran into the house.

"Shhh." Her father pointed to the radio.

Terri sat beside Jason on the couch near the window and listened. "Hurricane Hazel with its 90-mile-an-hour winds is almost upon us. The police have issued a warning to stay inside. Close all doors and windows."

The rain lashed against the roof. A gust of wind bent the little tree in their front yard to the ground. Terri watched the sky grow darker and darker.

"It's raining sideways," Jason whispered.

"And the street looks like a river." Terri spoke quietly, too.

Her mother moaned. "What if the house floods? We might have to evacuate. We might have to leave the house and go out in that storm."

"Wouldn't that be exciting!" Jason exclaimed.

But Terri wasn't so sure she wanted to go outside. She thought the wind might blow her away.

The overhead light in the room went out. The darkness made Terri feel as if she were suddenly standing in the middle of the storm.

"A power line must be down," her father said. "Better get some candles."

Terri followed everyone to the kitchen. The wind howled like a ghost. "Ooooohhhhh," Terri imitated, and shivers ran up her back. She looked

out the kitchen window at the backyard. All the leaves had blown off the
tree she'd been lying under.

Something white flew past the window.

"Bunbun!" Terri shrieked. The rabbit sailed into the wall of the
neighbor's house. But he didn't fall.
The wind held him spread-eagled
against the side of the house, three
feet off the ground.

Terri started to run outside to save
him. But she stopped herself. She
couldn't run out in a hurricane! She
dragged her father to the window and
pointed to the rabbit. "We can't just
leave him there!"

The whole family looked out the
window. Everyone was silent.

"What if I tie some sheets together,"
her mother said, "and let Jason out the
back door."

"Me?!!" Jason exclaimed.

Terri threw her arms around her mother. "Oh, Mom, would you?"

"I'll go," her father said.

"You are too big. We couldn't pull you back inside," her mother objected.

"But I thought you didn't like that old rabbit." Jason pulled on his mother's sleeve. Terri glared at him.

"I'm not going to let him die out there in a hurricane all alone," their mother answered. She pulled three sheets out of the linen closet in the hall.

"Why don't you just hang me by my big toe in the basement? Or drop me off the roof?" Jason asked. "But don't send me out there."

"It will be exciting, remember?" Their mother tied the sheets together.

Terri looked back and forth between the kitchen and the rabbit. Bunbun looked so small.

"Don't you love me?" Jason threw

his arms into the air. "I'm too young to die."

Terri couldn't tell if Jason was teasing. Her father laughed as he tied one end of the sheets around the boy's waist. Then her father unlatched the kitchen door. He leaned against it so it wouldn't fly open. The wind swooshed in. A potted plant crashed to the floor.

"But I'm your only son," Jason cried.

"Please," Terri pleaded. "Please hurry."

Jason gave her one despairing look and walked into the storm. The wind caught him and threw him against the wall next to Bunbun. Jason hesitated, then grabbed the rabbit.

"Help me, Terri." Her mother pulled on the sheets.

Jason stumbled. He struggled to stay on his feet, leaning into the wind. Then a gust whipped him sideways,

first one way and then the other. Jason fell, but he held on to Bunbun. He crawled on his knees and one hand. Terri and her mother pulled at the sheets, hand over hand. Her father grabbed Jason's arm and hauled him into the kitchen.

"Bunbun." Terri cradled the wet, trembling rabbit in her arms and nestled her face into his soggy fur. "Thank you, Jason."

Jason's soaked clothes stuck to his body. He waved an imaginary sword in the air. "Jason the mighty rabbit-saver strikes again!"

"Why does that rabbit always have to go to the bathroom in my house," her mother said.

Surprised, Terri looked down to see rabbit pellets dropping to the floor. "Ah, Mom, he's scared."

Cries in the Night

The day after Halloween, Terri awakened very early. She didn't feel sleepy anymore. Maybe she had eaten too much candy last night. Terri got out of bed, put on her robe and slippers, and knelt in front of her window. There was only one star left in the sky. She watched it fade.

"Star light, star bright /Last star I've seen tonight . . ./I wish I may, I wish I might /Have this wish I wish tonight," Terri recited, proud of the way she had changed the words. "I still wish that Bunbun could sleep with me."

She could barely see the corner of his run. It was empty. He must be asleep in his wooden house.

The lawn was covered with a film of white frost. Two animals raced across the yard. For a moment Terri thought they both looked like cats. But the first one had pure white fur, and it hopped. Bunbun was out of his cage! He was being chased by a big orange cat! The two animals ran around and around the lilac bushes. The cat moved closer to Bunbun.

Terri raced down the stairs to the back door. An animal screamed.

"I'll save you, Bunbun!" Terri yanked open the door and ran across the yard. Her slippers crunched on the frosty grass.

When she came to the lilac bushes, Terri slid to a stop, horrified. The neighbor's cat was stuck in a bush. Bunbun was kicking it with his back legs. Blood dripped down the cat's stomach.

Terri dove for the rabbit, but she missed and fell on her elbows on the hard ground. She chased Bunbun around the bush, tripping over her bathrobe. Bunbun kicked the cat again as he went by. Terri's heart pounded so fast she could feel it thumping inside her chest. She stopped in front of the cat and waited for Bunbun to come around again. The frantic cat raked its claws across the back of her ankle. Terri screamed.

"Jason! Jason!" She ran into the house and pulled her brother out of bed.

Jason hurried down the stairs after her. "Out of bed in the middle of the night for a rabbit," he mumbled. "First a hurricane. Now a cat fight."

Terri and Jason reached the lilac bushes. The neighbor came out in her nightgown.

Bunbun was kicking the cat again. Jason grabbed the rabbit, then screeched. "It bit me!" He stumbled into the bush, and the cat scratched him from his wrist to his elbow. "Here is your old rabbit," Jason yelled, throwing Bunbun at Terri. The rabbit chattered angrily in her arms.

The neighbor was crying. She knelt beside her cat and gently disentangled him from the bush. At least the cat was still alive.

Terri's parents came out the back door, and her mother grabbed Jason. "Jason, look at your arm!"

"Look at my cat!" the neighbor cried.

They all turned and stared at Terri.

"If you can't control that rabbit, you may not keep him," her mother said.

Buried Alive

Terri knew she would never forget what happened that night after Bunbun hurt the cat. Her parents told her that if the rabbit got out and caused trouble one more time, Terri would have to give him away. But Bunbun hadn't caused any more trouble. The ground had been frozen for months, so he couldn't dig out of his pen. It was January already.

Terri couldn't sleep. The wind howled, and her bedroom shutters rattled and creaked. She crept down the stairs in her nightgown. Maybe Dad would help her get a cup of hot chocolate.

Just as Terri crossed the dining room, the back door opened. Her mother swooshed into the kitchen. There was snow on her hair and shoulders.

Mother leaned up against the door and spread her arms out by her sides. "Well, I tried." She spoke to Dad, who was sitting at the kitchen table.

Terri felt as if she were watching a movie.

"I tried for twenty minutes in freezing weather to get that rabbit out of his cage," her mother exclaimed. "First he hopped this way and then he hopped that way, always just out of my reach."

Terri held her breath. Something was wrong. But she kept quiet.

Her father was quiet, too.

Mother flopped down in a chair. "If that rabbit wants to get buried alive in a blizzard, it's his own fault."

"A blizzard!" Terri cried.

Her mother jumped to her feet. "Terri, what are you doing out of bed?"

"I'll get Bunbun, Mom. He'll come to me!" Terri ran into the kitchen.

"I couldn't see a foot in front of me out there, Terri. You can't go out."

"What do you mean, I can't?" Terri snapped.

Her father's hand clamped down on her shoulder. "If your mother says it is snowing too hard, then you can't go out."

"Will you go?" she pleaded.

Her father answered gently, "That rabbit wouldn't come to me." Then his voice grew cold. "The last time I picked him up, he bit me. No, I won't go."

Terri faced her mother. "Then go out with me!"

"I spent twenty minutes freezing for

that rabbit, and I'm not going out again. You know it's dangerous in a blizzard."

Terri could tell her mother was angry, but Terri was angry, too. "How bad is the blizzard supposed to be? How much snow?"

Her parents were silent.

"Go to bed, Terri," her father said. "We'll look for him in the morning."

"He'll be dead by then!" Terri cried. She ran up the stairs and threw herself into bed. Then Terri thought about her parents. Her mother wanted Bunbun to die. She probably hadn't even tried to catch him. And her father didn't care.

The next morning, Terri awakened to see her mother standing over her bed. "Your father needs your help."

The room was just beginning to get light. Terri was confused. It was too early. She didn't want to get up.

"Look at the snow," her mother said.

Terri stumbled out of bed and opened the curtains. The snow sloped all the way up to her second-floor window. Terri had never seen so much snow. "Mom!" she exclaimed. "The road is gone, and the cars are gone!" Then she remembered. "And Bunbun's cage is gone!"

Her mother put her arm around her, but Terri pulled away.

"Terri, listen to me. Sometimes there is enough air in snow so that an animal can breathe."

Maybe Bunbun was alive! Terri grabbed her mother's hand.

"Your father is digging for him right now. He needs your help."

Terri had never dressed so fast in her whole life. Her mother met her in Jason's room with their snow clothes. Jason was going to help, too. They opened the window. Terri swung her feet over the ledge. She was two stories off the ground. Terri wondered how far she would sink in the fresh snow. Would she disappear over her head? But that was silly. Her father stood close by, only buried to his waist. The fresh snow must be wet and heavy. It would hold her up.

"Hurry, Terri. It's cold," her mother said.

Terri eased herself off the windowsill into the snow. She sunk to her middle. Her mother handed her a shovel, and Terri waded over to her father. He was digging next to the house.

"You dig farther away from the house," he said. "We'll cut a hole in the cage with wire cutters when we get there."

Jason jumped out of the window. "Finding a white rabbit in snow will be like trying to find a mouse in a field of mushrooms."

Their father laughed. "Two of us are enough to dig for the rabbit. You try to find the car."

The cold air burned the inside of Terri's nose, and she breathed out billows of frost. She scooped a shovelful of snow. It was hard to dig when

she was standing buried almost to her waist.

Jason pushed the handle of his shovel into the snow over and over again. His shoulders were bent. "Twenty years of hard labor," he moaned. "All I did was steal a loaf of bread. Is there no justice for a starving boy?"

How could Jason make jokes? Bunbun might be dead. Out of the corner of her eye, Terri thought she saw a blob of snow shift. She stared, but nothing moved. She and her father hadn't even dug to the top of the kitchen window yet. How could they ever get to Bunbun in time?

"Hot chocolate and muffins." Her mother leaned out of Jason's window.

Jason shoved his handle into the snow, hard. *Tink.* "Hey, listen!" *Tink.* *Tink.* "I found the car."

"Good boy," her father said. "Now

you get to dig for it."

Jason dropped his shovel. "Even people sentenced to hard labor get to eat."

Terri stared across the yard. She had seen the snow bounce again. There it was! "Mom, look!" The snow hopped one, two, three times! Then Terri saw two pink eyes. "Bunbun!"

The rabbit hopped slowly toward them. His pink nose twitched.

"That's impossible!" her mother exclaimed.

"The ground is hard as rock," Jason said. "He couldn't have dug out."

"Anything is possible for the mighty Bunbun," Terri answered. "Hey, he'll have to stay inside for a few days. He'll have to sleep with me."

"I'm beginning to think you have a magic rabbit," her father said.

"Bunbun, the mighty magic bunny!" Terri laughed. Jason groaned.

Bunbun Rides Again

Spring was the perfect time for a circus. Terri planned to invite everyone in the neighborhood.

"You hold Sonya," Terri said to her younger friend, David. He obediently hooked his hand into his dog's collar.

"We're going to have the greatest show on earth." Terri let Bunbun out of his cage. The snow had completely disappeared, and Terri wore only jeans and a light sweater. Bunbun stood up on his back legs and sniffed the air. He ignored the dog. Sonya came over to visit his pen almost every day.

"Bunbun Rides Again," Terri said.

"That's a good name for the act."

David nodded.

"Maybe this act will be so good that Bunbun will become famous," Terri said. "Then even my mother will like him."

"Maybe he'll join the Barnum and Bailey circus." David struggled to hold on to Sonya.

"And I could be his trainer." Terri picked up Bunbun. "Come on, let's go inside. Sonya will just run away out here."

"Won't your mother get mad?" David asked.

"She's next door having a cup of tea." Terri tried to stand taller and look more important. "She won't mind. This is special. Bunbun might become a star." Terri wasn't so sure her mother would agree, but she was too excited to care.

Triumphantly, Terri carried Bunbun

into the house, as if she were in a parade. David dragged Sonya up the stairs behind her.

'We'll practice in the dining room," Terri said. "Now you get ready to let Sonya go on the count of three. One. Two . . ." Terri put Bunbun down on Sonya's shoulders. "Three!"

The dog twirled around in a circle as if she were chasing her tail. Bunbun slipped off.

Terri and David laughed. "Come on, let's try again," Terri said, and reached for Bunbun. But the rabbit hopped away. She chased him back and forth across the room in quick little steps until she cornered him. David hauled Sonya out from under the table. The dog's tail was between her legs.

"Okay. One. Two. Three!" Terri put the rabbit down on Sonya's shoulders again. This time Sonya shot in a straight line into the living room. Bunbun stayed on for a few seconds and then rolled off, backward. He landed on his tail on the floor. Sonya ran around and around the room, barking.

Terri laughed, even though she could tell Bunbun was angry. He chattered his front teeth together and twitched his nose furiously.

"Let's try again." David swooped down on the rabbit.

"No, David," Terri cried. But David didn't listen. He grabbed the rabbit and began running toward Sonya.

"Put him down!" Terri ran after him.

Bunbun kicked at David's arm and bit his finger. David screamed and dropped the rabbit.

"I told you not to pick him up," Terri yelled. David began sobbing. Blood dripped from his hand.

"What's going on?" Terri's mother burst into the room.

Terri looked at her mother, horrified. Her mother looked at the dog, at the rabbit, and at David's bleeding hand. Then she put her arm around the boy and led him out of the room.

Good-bye

"Wherever there's a rabbit, there'll be rabbit droppings." Jason helped Terri clean up the mess Sonya and Bunbun had made in the dining room. Their parents talked in the kitchen. Terri knew Jason was trying to cheer her up, but she didn't feel like being happy.

Her brother leaned down beside the chair and picked up a shoe. "Look, Bunbun went to the bathroom in Mom's shoe."

Terri stopped sweeping and smiled a little. The door from the kitchen opened.

"Come here, Terri," her father said.

Terri stumbled after him. Her knees wobbled like jelly, and her stomach felt sick.

"Terri," her mother began, "we told you when Bunbun hurt the cat that if he caused trouble one more time he would have to go." Her mother looked unhappy. Terri started crying.

"He's caused trouble one more time, Terri, and he has to go."

Terri looked at her father. "He's not safe, honey," he said. "He hurts other animals and he bites people. The ground is soft again. He'll be digging out all the time."

Terri nodded. She was losing her Bunbun. Her father put his arm around her. Terri leaned her head against his shoulder and sobbed. "Where will he go, Daddy?"

"I'll take him to the vet tomorrow morning," her mother said.

Terri jerked away from her father's shoulder. Suddenly she didn't feel sad anymore, only terrified.

"The vet will have to put him to sleep, Terri," her mother said softly.

"Does that mean kill him?" Terri's whole body stiffened.

Her mother nodded.

Terri threw herself at her mother and pounded at her with her fists. "You can't kill Bunbun! You can't kill Bunbun!" she screamed.

Her father grabbed Terri away. He held her arms so hard they hurt. "Where can he go?" he said angrily. "We can't find a home for him. Who would take a biting rabbit? He bites, Terri. Don't you understand?" Her father had never really shouted at her before.

Terri stood still until he let go of her arms. Then she bolted out of the kitchen and ran to her room. She slammed her door and dragged her desk in front of it.

No one called her for dinner that night. Jason knocked on her door, but she didn't answer. A little later, Terri came downstairs and stood by her mother's chair. She touched her on the shoulder. "I'm sorry, Mom." Terri tried to keep from sobbing again. "I didn't mean to hit you."

"I'm sorry, too." Her mother put her arm around Terri. She looked sad. "Do you want some dinner?"

Terri shook her head and climbed

back up the stairs to her bedroom. Somehow she had to help Bunbun. There must be some way besides killing him. He wasn't that dangerous.

Terri heard Jason go to bed. But she stayed awake. Sometimes she thought about Bunbun and part of the time she just stared.

A few hours later Terri woke up in a cramped position. She had fallen asleep. It was still dark outside, but the birds were beginning to sing.

Bunbun! Terri's lungs stiffened inside of her, and for a moment she felt as if she couldn't breathe. She went to the window and looked out at the backyard. Bunbun liked hopping through the grass so much. She wished she could send him somewhere where there was grass.

The park! She could take Bunbun to the park. Why hadn't she thought of it before? Terri ran into Jason's room and shook him awake.

"Wake up, Jason. We're going to take Bunbun to his new home. Please help me."

Slowly, Jason woke up and listened to her plan.

"I'll help," he said. He dressed and followed her downstairs to the rabbit cage.

"I'll get the wagon out from the garage," Jason said.

Terri pulled Bunbun's wooden hutch out of the wire run. When Jason returned, they set the little house in the wagon. Then Terri crawled into the wire run to get Bunbun. She squeezed him tightly against her and put him in his hutch.

Terri and Jason carried the wagon until they were past the house, so the wheels wouldn't squeak. The sky was just beginning to lighten. They walked over a mile to the park. By the time they got there, the sun was up.

In the middle of the park, by the duck pond, was a rabbit pen. Cement had been poured around the edge of the pen so the rabbits couldn't dig out, and a strong wire fence stood about six feet high. Wire covered the top, too. But in one corner of the top there was a hole, not big enough to climb through, but big enough to drop a rabbit in.

"We have to hurry," Jason said. "Someone may come."

Terri climbed up and sat on top of the fence. Carefully, Jason picked up

Bunbun by the back of the neck and under his bottom, so the rabbit couldn't bite. Jason handed Bunbun up to Terri.

She cradled him in her arms and nuzzled her face down in his fur. "Don't be afraid," she said softly. "I'll come visit you every day."

Then Terri picked Bunbun up by the back of the neck and dropped him into the cage. She hoped the fall wouldn't hurt him. Bunbun hopped into a corner and froze. A white rabbit with black spots hopped over to him and twitched its nose. Then it moved away. Bunbun followed the rabbit over to a pile of food and began eating.

"Come on, Terri. We have to go," Jason said.

Terri scrambled down off the fence and pressed her face against the wire. "Good-bye, Bunbun," she whispered.